Tom Tiddler's Ground

Charles Dickens

Contents

TOM TIDDLER'S GROUND

BY

Charles Dickens

TOM TIDDLER'S GROUND
CHAPTER I--PICKING UP SOOT AND CINDERS

"And why Tom Tiddler's ground?" said the Traveller.

"Because he scatters halfpence to Tramps and such-like," returned the Landlord, "and of course they pick 'em up. And this being done on his own land (which it *is* his own land, you observe, and were his family's before him), why it is but regarding the halfpence as gold and silver, and turning the ownership of the property a bit round your finger, and there you have the name of the children's game complete. And it's appropriate too," said the Landlord, with his favourite action of stooping a little, to look across the table out of window at vacancy, under the window-blind which was half drawn down. "Leastwise it has been so considered by many gentlemen which have partook of chops and tea in the present humble parlour."

The Traveller was partaking of chops and tea in the present humble parlour, and the Landlord's shot was fired obliquely at him.

"And you call him a Hermit?" said the Traveller.

"They call him such," returned the Landlord, evading personal responsibility; "he is in general so considered."

"What *is* a Hermit?" asked the Traveller.

"What is it?" repeated the Landlord, drawing his hand across his chin.

"Yes, what is it?"

The Landlord stooped again, to get a more comprehensive view of vacancy under the window-blind, and--with an asphyxiated appearance on him as one unaccustomed to definition--made no answer.

"I'll tell you what I suppose it to be," said the Traveller. "An abominably dirty thing."

"Mr. Mopes is dirty, it cannot be denied," said the Landlord.

"Intolerably conceited."

"Mr. Mopes is vain of the life he leads, some do say," replied the Landlord, as another concession.

"A slothful, unsavoury, nasty reversal of the laws of human mature," said the Traveller; "and for the sake of GOD'S working world and its wholesomeness, both moral and physical, I would put the thing on the treadmill (if I had my way) wherever I found it; whether on a pillar, or in a hole; whether on Tom Tiddler's ground, or the Pope of Rome's ground, or a Hindoo fakeer's ground, or any other ground."

"I don't know about putting Mr. Mopes on the treadmill," said the Landlord, shaking his head very seriously. "There ain't a doubt but what he has got landed property."

"How far may it be to this said Tom Tiddler's ground?" asked the Traveller.

"Put it at five mile," returned the Landlord.

"Well! When I have done my breakfast," said the Traveller, "I'll go there. I came over here this morning, to find it out and see it."

"Many does," observed the Landlord.

The conversation passed, in the Midsummer weather of no remote year of grace, down among the pleasant dales and trout-streams of a green English county. No matter what county. Enough that you may hunt there, shoot there, fish there, traverse long grass-grown Roman roads there, open ancient barrows there, see many a square mile of richly cultivated land there, and hold Arcadian talk with a bold peasantry, their country's pride, who will tell you (if you want to know) how pastoral housekeeping is done on nine shillings a week.

Mr. Traveller sat at his breakfast in the little sanded parlour of the Peal of Bells village alehouse, with the dew and dust of an early walk upon his shoes--an early walk by road and meadow and coppice, that had sprinkled him bountifully with little blades of grass, and scraps of new hay, and with leaves both young and old, and with other such fragrant tokens of the freshness and wealth of summer. The window through which the landlord had concentrated his gaze upon vacancy was shaded, because the morning sun was hot and bright on the village street. The village street was like most other village streets: wide for its height, silent for its size, and drowsy in the dullest degree. The quietest little dwellings with the largest of window-shutters (to shut up Nothing as carefully as if it were the Mint, or the Bank of England) had called in the Doctor's house so suddenly, that his brass door-plate and three stories stood among them as conspicuous and different as the doctor himself in his broadcloth, among the smock-frocks of his patients. The village residences seemed to have gone to law with a similar absence of consideration, for a score of weak little lath-and-plaster cabins clung in confusion about the Attorney's red-brick house, which, with glaring door-steps and a most terrific scraper, seemed to serve all manner of ejectments upon them. They were as various as labourers--high-shouldered, wry-necked, one-eyed, goggle-eyed, squinting, bow-legged, knock-knee'd, rheumatic, crazy. Some of the small tradesmen's houses, such as the crockery-shop and the harness-maker, had a Cyclops window in the middle of the gable, within an inch or two of its apex, suggesting that some forlorn rural Prentice must wriggle himself into that apartment horizontally, when he retired to rest, after the manner of the worm. So bountiful in its abundance was the surrounding country, and so lean and scant the village, that one might have thought the village had sown and planted everything it once possessed, to convert the same into crops. This would account for the bareness of the little shops, the bareness of the few boards and trestles designed for market purposes in a corner of the street, the bareness of the obsolete Inn and Inn Yard, with the ominous inscription "Excise Office" not yet faded out from the gateway, as indicating the very last thing that poverty could get rid of. This would also account for the determined abandonment of the village by one stray dog, fast lessening in the perspective where the white posts and the pond were, and would explain his conduct on the hypothesis that he was going (through the act of suicide) to convert himself into manure, and become a part proprietor in turnips or mangold-wurzel.

Mr. Traveller having finished his breakfast and paid his moderate score, walked out to the threshold of the Peal of Bells, and, thence directed by the pointing finger of his host, betook himself towards the ruined hermitage of Mr. Mopes the hermit.

For, Mr. Mopes, by suffering everything about him to go to ruin, and by dressing himself in a blanket and skewer, and by steeping himself in soot and grease and other nastiness, had acquired great renown in all that country-side--far greater renown than he could ever have won for himself, if his career had been that of any ordinary Christian, or decent Hottentot. He had even blanketed and skewered and sooted and greased himself, into the London papers. And it was curious to find, as

Mr. Traveller found by stopping for a new direction at this farm-house or at that cottage as he went along, with how much accuracy the morbid Mopes had counted on the weakness of his neighbours to embellish him. A mist of home-brewed marvel and romance surrounded Mopes, in which (as in all fogs) the real proportions of the real object were extravagantly heightened. He had murdered his beautiful beloved in a fit of jealousy and was doing penance; he had made a vow under the influence of grief; he had made a vow under the influence of a fatal accident; he had made a vow under the influence of religion; he had made a vow under the influence of drink; he had made a vow under the influence of disappointment; he had never made any vow, but "had got led into it" by the possession of a mighty and most awful secret; he was enormously rich, he was stupendously charitable, he was profoundly learned, he saw spectres, he knew and could do all kinds of wonders. Some said he went out every night, and was met by terrified wayfarers stalking along dark roads, others said he never went out, some knew his penance to be nearly expired, others had positive information that his seclusion was not a penance at all, and would never expire but with himself. Even, as to the easy facts of how old he was, or how long he had held verminous occupation of his blanket and skewer, no consistent information was to be got, from those who must know if they would. He was represented as being all the ages between five-and-twenty and sixty, and as having been a hermit seven years, twelve, twenty, thirty,--though twenty, on the whole, appeared the favourite term.

"Well, well!" said Mr. Traveller. "At any rate, let us see what a real live Hermit looks like."

So, Mr. Traveller went on, and on, and on, until he came to Tom Tiddler's Ground.

It was a nook in a rustic by-road, which the genius of Mopes had laid waste as completely, as if he had been born an Emperor and a Conqueror. Its centre object was a dwelling-house, sufficiently substantial, all the window-glass of which had been long ago abolished by the surprising genius of Mopes, and all the windows of which were barred across with rough-split logs of trees nailed over them on the outside. A rickyard, hip-high in vegetable rankness and ruin, contained outbuildings from which the thatch had lightly fluttered away, on all the winds of all the seasons of the year, and from which the planks and beams had heavily dropped and rotted. The frosts and damps of winter, and the heats of summer, had warped what wreck remained, so that not a post or a board retained the position it was meant to hold, but everything was twisted from its purpose, like its owner, and degraded and debased. In this homestead of the sluggard, behind the ruined hedge, and sinking away among the ruined grass and the nettles, were the last perishing fragments of certain ricks: which had gradually mildewed and collapsed, until they looked like mounds of rotten honeycomb, or dirty sponge. Tom Tiddler's ground could even show its ruined water; for, there was a slimy pond into which a tree or two had fallen--one soppy trunk and branches lay across it then--which in its accumulation of stagnant weed, and in its black decomposition, and in all its foulness and filth, was almost comforting, regarded as the only water that could have reflected the shameful place without seeming polluted by that low office.

Mr. Traveller looked all around him on Tom Tiddler's ground, and his glance at last encountered a dusky Tinker lying among the weeds and rank grass, in the shade of the dwelling-house. A rough walking-staff lay on the ground by his side, and his head rested on a small wallet. He met Mr. Traveller's eye without lifting up his head, merely depressing his chin a little (for he was lying on his back) to get a better view of him.

"Good day!" said Mr. Traveller.

"Same to you, if you like it," returned the Tinker.

"Don't *you* like it? It's a very fine day."

"I ain't partickler in weather," returned the Tinker, with a yawn.

Mr. Traveller had walked up to where he lay, and was looking down at him. "This is a curious place," said Mr. Traveller.

"Ay, I suppose so!" returned the Tinker. "Tom Tiddler's ground, they call this."

"Are you well acquainted with it?"

"Never saw it afore to-day," said the Tinker, with another yawn, "and don't care if I never see it again. There was a man here just now, told me what it was called. If you want to see Tom himself, you must go in at that gate." He faintly indicated with his chin a little mean ruin of a wooden gate at the side of the house.

"Have you seen Tom?"

"No, and I ain't partickler to see him. I can see a dirty man anywhere."

"He does not live in the house, then?" said Mr. Traveller, casting his eyes upon the house anew.

"The man said," returned the Tinker, rather irritably,--"him as was here just now, 'this what you're a laying on, mate, is Tom Tiddler's ground. And if you want to see Tom,' he says, 'you must go in at that gate.' The man come out at that gate himself, and he ought to know."

"Certainly," said Mr. Traveller.

"Though, perhaps," exclaimed the Tinker, so struck by the brightness of his own idea, that it had the electric effect upon him of causing him to lift up his head an inch or so, "perhaps he was a liar! He told some rum 'uns--him as was here just now, did about this place of Tom's. He says--him as was here just now--'When Tom shut up the house, mate, to go to rack, the beds was left, all made, like as if somebody was a-going to sleep in every bed. And if you was to walk through the bedrooms now, you'd see the ragged mouldy bedclothes a heaving and a heaving like seas. And a heaving and a heaving with what?' he says. 'Why, with the rats under 'em.'"

"I wish I had seen that man," Mr. Traveller remarked.

"You'd have been welcome to see him instead of me seeing him," growled the Tinker; "for he was a long-winded one."

Not without a sense of injury in the remembrance, the Tinker gloomily closed his eyes. Mr. Traveller, deeming the Tinker a short-winded one, from whom no further breath of information was to be derived, betook himself to the gate.

Swung upon its rusty hinges, it admitted him into a yard in which there was nothing to be seen but an outhouse attached to the ruined building, with a barred window in it. As there were traces of many recent footsteps under this window, and as it was a low window, and unglazed, Mr. Traveller made bold to peep within the bars. And there to be sure he had a real live Hermit before him, and could judge how the real dead Hermits used to look.

He was lying on a bank of soot and cinders, on the floor, in front of a rusty fireplace. There was nothing else in the dark little kitchen, or scullery, or whatever his den had been originally used as, but a table with a litter of old bottles on it. A rat made a clatter among these bottles, jumped down, and ran over the real live Hermit on his way to his hole, or the man in *his* hole would not have been so easily discernible. Tickled in the face by the rat's tail, the owner of Tom Tiddler's ground opened his eyes, saw Mr. Traveller, started up, and sprang to the window.

"Humph!" thought Mr. Traveller, retiring a pace or two from the bars. "A compound of Newgate, Bedlam, a Debtors' Prison in the worst time, a chimney-sweep, a mudlark, and the Noble Savage! A nice old family, the Hermit family. Hah!"

Mr. Traveller thought this, as he silently confronted the sooty object in the blanket and skewer (in sober truth it wore nothing else), with the matted hair and the staring eyes. Further, Mr. Traveller thought, as the eye surveyed him with a very obvious curiosity in ascertaining the effect they produced, "Vanity, vanity, vanity! Verily, all is vanity!"

"What is your name, sir, and where do you come from?" asked Mr. Mopes the Hermit--with an air of authority, but in the ordinary human speech of one who has been to school.

Mr. Traveller answered the inquiries.

"Did you come here, sir, to see *me*?"

"I did. I heard of you, and I came to see you.--I know you like to be seen." Mr. Traveller coolly threw the last words in, as a matter of course, to forestall an affectation of resentment or objection that he saw rising beneath the grease and grime of the face. They had their effect.

"So," said the Hermit, after a momentary silence, unclasping the bars by which he had previously held, and seating himself behind them on the ledge of the window, with his bare legs and feet crouched up, "you know I like to be seen?"

Mr. Traveller looked about him for something to sit on, and, observing a billet of wood in a corner, brought it near the window. Deliberately seating himself upon it, he answered, "Just so."

Each looked at the other, and each appeared to take some pains to get the measure of the other.

"Then you have come to ask me why I lead this life," said the Hermit, frowning in a stormy manner. "I never tell that to any human being. I will not be asked that."

"Certainly you will not be asked that by me," said Mr. Traveller, "for I have not the slightest desire to know."

"You are an uncouth man," said Mr. Mopes the Hermit.

"You are another," said Mr. Traveller.

The Hermit, who was plainly in the habit of overawing his visitors with the novelty of his filth and his blanket and skewer, glared at his present visitor in some discomfiture and surprise: as if he had taken aim at him with a sure gun, and his piece had missed fire.

"Why do you come here at all?" he asked, after a pause.

"Upon my life," said Mr. Traveller, "I was made to ask myself that very question only a few minutes ago--by a Tinker too."

As he glanced towards the gate in saying it, the Hermit glanced in that direction likewise.

"Yes. He is lying on his back in the sunlight outside," said Mr, Traveller, as if he had been asked concerning the man, "and he won't come in; for he says--and really very reasonably--'What should I come in for? I can see a dirty man anywhere.'"

"You are an insolent person. Go away from my premises. Go!" said the Hermit, in an imperious and angry tone.

"Come, come!" returned Mr. Traveller, quite undisturbed. "This is a little too much. You are not going to call yourself clean? Look at your legs. And as to these being your premises:--they are in far too disgraceful a condition to claim any privilege of ownership, or anything else."

The Hermit bounced down from his window-ledge, and cast himself on his bed of soot and cinders.

"I am not going," said Mr. Traveller, glancing in after him; "you won't get rid of me in that way. You had better come and talk."

"I won't talk," said the Hermit, flouncing round to get his back towards the window.

"Then I will," said Mr. Traveller. "Why should you take it ill that I have no curiosity to know why you live this highly absurd and highly indecent life? When I contemplate a man in a state of disease, surely there is no moral obligation on me to be anxious to know how he took it."

After a short silence, the Hermit bounced up again, and came back to the barred window.

"What? You are not gone?" he said, affecting to have supposed that he was.

"Nor going," Mr. Traveller replied: "I design to pass this summer day here."

"How dare you come, sir, upon my promises--" the Hermit was returning, when his visitor interrupted him.

"Really, you know, you must *not* talk about your premises. I cannot allow such a place as this to be dignified with the name of premises."

"How dare you," said the Hermit, shaking his bars, "come in at my gate, to taunt me with being in a diseased state?"

"Why, Lord bless my soul," returned the other, very composedly, "you have not the face to say that you are in a wholesome state? Do allow me again to call your attention to your legs. Scrape yourself anywhere--with anything--and then tell me you are in a wholesome state. The fact is, Mr. Mopes, that you are not only a Nuisance--"

"A Nuisance?" repeated the Hermit, fiercely.

"What is a place in this obscene state of dilapidation but a Nuisance? What is a man in your obscene state of dilapidation but a Nuisance? Then, as you very well know, you cannot do without an audience, and your audience is a Nuisance. You attract all the disreputable vagabonds and prowlers within ten miles around, by exhibiting yourself to them in that objectionable blanket, and by throwing copper money among them, and giving them drink out of those very dirty jars and bottles that I see in there (their stomachs need be strong!); and in short," said Mr. Traveller, summing up in a quietly and comfortably settled manner, "you are a Nuisance, and this kennel is a Nuisance, and the audience that you cannot possibly dispense with is a Nuisance, and the Nuisance is not merely a local Nuisance, because it is a general Nuisance to know that there *can be* such a Nuisance left in civilisation so very long after its time."

"Will you go away? I have a gun in here," said the Hermit.

"Pooh!"

"I *have*!"

"Now, I put it to you. Did I say you had not? And as to going away, didn't I say I am not going away? You have made me forget where I was. I now remember that I was remarking on your conduct being a Nuisance. Moreover, it is in the last and lowest degree inconsequent foolishness and weakness."

"Weakness?" echoed the Hermit.

"Weakness," said Mr. Traveller, with his former comfortably settled final air.

"I weak, you fool?" cried the Hermit, "I, who have held to my purpose, and my diet, and my only bed there, all these years?"

"The more the years, the weaker you," returned Mr. Traveller. "Though the years are not so many as folks say, and as you willingly take credit for. The crust upon your face is thick and dark, Mr. Mopes, but I can see enough of you through it, to see that you are still a young man."

"Inconsequent foolishness is lunacy, I suppose?" said the Hermit.

"I suppose it is very like it," answered Mr. Traveller.

"Do I converse like a lunatic?"

"One of us two must have a strong presumption against him of being one, whether or no. Either the clean and decorously clad man, or the dirty and indecorously clad man. I don't say which."

"Why, you self-sufficient bear," said the Hermit, "not a day passes but I am justified in my purpose by the conversations I hold here; not a day passes but I am shown, by everything I hear and see here, how right and strong I am in holding my purpose."

Mr. Traveller, lounging easily on his billet of wood, took out a pocket pipe and began to fill it. "Now, that a man," he said, appealing to the summer sky as he did so, "that a man--even behind bars, in a blanket and skewer--should tell me that he can see, from day to day, any orders or conditions of men, women, or children, who can by any possibility teach him that it is anything but the miserablest drivelling for a human creature to quarrel with his social nature--not to go so far as to say, to renounce his common human decency, for that is an extreme case; or who can teach him that he can in any wise separate himself from his kind and the habits of his kind, without becoming a deteriorated spectacle calculated to give the Devil (and perhaps the monkeys) pleasure,--is something wonderful! I repeat," said Mr. Traveller, beginning to smoke, "the unreasoning hardihood of it is something wonderful--even in a man with the dirt upon him an inch or two thick--behind bars--in a blanket and skewer!"

The Hermit looked at him irresolutely, and retired to his soot and cinders and lay down, and got up again and came to the bars, and again looked at him irresolutely, and finally said with sharpness: "I don't like tobacco."

"I don't like dirt," rejoined Mr. Traveller; "tobacco is an excellent disinfectant.

We shall both be the better for my pipe. It is my intention to sit here through this summer day, until that blessed summer sun sinks low in the west, and to show you what a poor creature you are, through the lips of every chance wayfarer who may come in at your gate."

"What do you mean?" inquired the Hermit, with a furious air.

"I mean that yonder is your gate, and there are you, and here am I; I mean that I know it to be a moral impossibility that any person can stray in at that gate from any point of the compass, with any sort of experience, gained at first hand, or derived from another, that can confute me and justify you."

"You are an arrogant and boastful hero," said the Hermit. "You think yourself profoundly wise."

"Bah!" returned Mr. Traveller, quietly smoking. "There is little wisdom in knowing that every man must be up and doing, and that all mankind are made dependent on one another."

"You have companions outside," said the Hermit. "I am not to be imposed upon by your assumed confidence in the people who may enter."

"A depraved distrust," returned the visitor, compassionately raising his eyebrows, "of course belongs to your state, I can't help that."

"Do you mean to tell me you have no confederates?"

"I mean to tell you nothing but what I have told you. What I have told you is, that it is a moral impossibility that any son or daughter of Adam can stand on this ground that I put my foot on, or on any ground that mortal treads, and gainsay the healthy tenure on which we hold our existence."

"Which is," sneered the Hermit, "according to you--"

"Which is," returned the other, "according to Eternal Providence, that we must arise and wash our faces and do our gregarious work and act and re- act on one another, leaving only the idiot and the palsied to sit blinking in the corner. Come!" apostrophising the gate. "Open Sesame! Show his eyes and grieve his heart! I don't care who comes, for I know what must come of it!"

With that, he faced round a little on his billet of wood towards the gate; and Mr. Mopes, the Hermit, after two or three ridiculous bounces of indecision at his bed and back again, submitted to what he could not help himself against, and coiled himself on his window-ledge, holding to his bars and looking out rather anxiously.

CHAPTER VI--PICKING UP MISS KIMMEENS {1}

The day was by this time waning, when the gate again opened, and, with the brilliant golden light that streamed from the declining sun and touched the very bars of the sooty creature's den, there passed in a little child; a little girl with beautiful bright hair. She wore a plain straw hat, had a door-key in her hand, and tripped towards Mr. Traveller as if she were pleased to see him and were going to repose some childish confidence in him, when she caught sight of the figure behind the bars, and started back in terror.

"Don't be alarmed, darling!" said Mr. Traveller, taking her by the hand.

"Oh, but I don't like it!" urged the shrinking child; "it's dreadful."

"Well! I don't like it either," said Mr. Traveller.

"Who has put it there?" asked the little girl. "Does it bite?"

"No,--only barks. But can't you make up your mind to see it, my dear?" For she was covering her eyes.

"O no no no!" returned the child. "I cannot bear to look at it!"

Mr. Traveller turned his head towards his friend in there, as much as to ask him how he liked that instance of his success, and then took the child out at the still open gate, and stood talking to her for some half an hour in the mellow sunlight. At length he returned, encouraging her as she held his arm with both her hands; and laying his protecting hand upon her head and smoothing her pretty hair, he addressed his friend behind the bars as follows:

      * * * * *

Miss Pupford's establishment for six young ladies of tender years, is an establishment of a compact nature, an establishment in miniature, quite a pocket establishment. Miss Pupford, Miss Pupford's assistant with the Parisian accent, Miss Pupford's cook, and Miss Pupford's housemaid, complete what Miss Pupford calls the educational and domestic staff of her Lilliputian College.

Miss Pupford is one of the most amiable of her sex; it necessarily follows that she possesses a sweet temper, and would own to the possession of a great deal of sentiment if she considered it quite reconcilable with her duty to parents. Deeming it not in the bond, Miss Pupford keeps it as far out of sight as she can--which (God bless her!) is not very far.

Miss Pupford's assistant with the Parisian accent, may be regarded as in some sort an inspired lady, for she never conversed with a Parisian, and was never out of England--except once in the pleasure-boat Lively, in the foreign waters that ebb and flow two miles off Margate at high water. Even under those geographically favourable circumstances for the acquisition of the French language in its utmost politeness and purity, Miss Pupford's assistant did not fully profit by the opportunity; for the pleasure-boat, Lively, so strongly asserted its title to its name on that occasion, that she was reduced to the condition of lying in the bottom of the boat pickling in brine--as if she were being salted down for the use of the Navy--undergoing at the same time great mental alarm, corporeal distress, and clear-starching derangement.

When Miss Pupford and her assistant first foregathered, is not known to men, or pupils. But, it was long ago. A belief would have established itself among pupils that the two once went to school together, were it not for the difficulty and audacity of imagining Miss Pupford born without mittens, and without a front, and without a bit of gold wire among her front teeth, and without little dabs of powder on her neat little face and nose. Indeed, whenever Miss Pupford gives a little lecture on the mythology of the misguided heathens (always carefully excluding Cupid from recognition), and tells how Minerva sprang, perfectly equipped, from the brain of Jupiter, she is half supposed to hint, "So I myself came into the world, completely up in Pinnock, Mangnall, Tables, and the use of the Globes."

Howbeit, Miss Pupford and Miss Pupford's assistant are old old friends. And it is thought by pupils that, after pupils are gone to bed, they even call one another by their christian names in the quiet little parlour. For, once upon a time on a thunderous afternoon, when Miss Pupford fainted away without notice, Miss Pupford's assistant (never heard, before or since, to address her otherwise than as Miss Pupford) ran to her, crying out, "My dearest Euphemia!" And Euphemia is Miss Pupford's christian name on the sampler (date picked out) hanging up in the College- hall, where the two peacocks, terrified to death by some German text that is waddling down-hill after them out of a cottage, are scuttling away to hide their profiles in two immense bean-stalks growing out of flower-pots.

Also, there is a notion latent among pupils, that Miss Pupford was once in love, and that the beloved object still moves upon this ball. Also, that he is a public character, and a personage of vast consequence. Also, that Miss Pupford's assistant knows all about it. For, sometimes of an afternoon when Miss Pupford has been reading the paper through her little gold eye-glass (it is necessary to read it on the spot, as the boy calls for it, with ill-conditioned punctuality, in an hour), she has become agitated, and has said to her assistant "G!" Then Miss Pupford's assistant has gone to Miss Pupford, and Miss Pupford has pointed out, with her eye-glass, G in the paper, and then Miss Pupford's assistant has read about G, and has shown sympathy. So stimulated has the pupil-mind been in its time to curiosity on the subject of G, that once, under temporary circumstances favourable to the bold sally, one fearless pupil did actually obtain possession of the paper, and range all over it in search of G, who had been discovered therein by Miss Pupford not ten minutes before. But no G could be identified, except one capital offender who had been executed in a state of great hardihood, and it was not to be supposed that Miss Pupford could ever have loved *him*. Besides, he couldn't be always being executed. Besides, he got into the paper again, alive, within a month.

On the whole, it is suspected by the pupil-mind that G is a short chubby old gentleman, with little black sealing-wax boots up to his knees, whom a sharply observant pupil, Miss Linx, when she once went to Tunbridge Wells with Miss Pupford for the holidays, reported on her return (privately and confidentially) to have seen come capering up to Miss Pupford on the Promenade, and to have detected in the act of squeezing Miss Pupford's hand, and to have heard pronounce the words, "Cruel Euphemia, ever thine!"--or something like that. Miss Linx hazarded a guess that he might be House of Commons, or Money Market, or Court Circular, or Fashionable Movements; which would account for his getting into the paper so often. But, it was fatally objected by the pupil-mind, that none of those notabilities could possibly be spelt with a G.

There are other occasions, closely watched and perfectly comprehended by the pupil-mind, when Miss Pupford imparts with mystery to her assistant that there is special excitement in the morning paper. These occasions are, when Miss Pupford finds an old pupil coming out under the head of Births, or Marriages. Affectionate tears are invariably seen in Miss Pupford's meek little eyes when this is the case;

and the pupil-mind, perceiving that its order has distinguished itself--though the fact is never mentioned by Miss Pupford--becomes elevated, and feels that it likewise is reserved for greatness.

Miss Pupford's assistant with the Parisian accent has a little more bone than Miss Pupford, but is of the same trim orderly diminutive cast, and, from long contemplation, admiration, and imitation of Miss Pupford, has grown like her. Being entirely devoted to Miss Pupford, and having a pretty talent for pencil-drawing, she once made a portrait of that lady: which was so instantly identified and hailed by the pupils, that it was done on stone at five shillings. Surely the softest and milkiest stone that ever was quarried, received that likeness of Miss Pupford! The lines of her placid little nose are so undecided in it that strangers to the work of art are observed to be exceedingly perplexed as to where the nose goes to, and involuntarily feel their own noses in a disconcerted manner. Miss Pupford being represented in a state of dejection at an open window, ruminating over a bowl of gold fish, the pupil-mind has settled that the bowl was presented by G, and that he wreathed the bowl with flowers of soul, and that Miss Pupford is depicted as waiting for him on a memorable occasion when he was behind his time.

The approach of the last Midsummer holidays had a particular interest for the pupil-mind, by reason of its knowing that Miss Pupford was bidden, on the second day of those holidays, to the nuptials of a former pupil. As it was impossible to conceal the fact--so extensive were the dress-making preparations--Miss Pupford openly announced it. But, she held it due to parents to make the announcement with an air of gentle melancholy, as if marriage were (as indeed it exceptionally has been) rather a calamity. With an air of softened resignation and pity, therefore, Miss Pupford went on with her preparations: and meanwhile no pupil ever went up-stairs, or came down, without peeping in at the door of Miss Pupford's bedroom (when Miss Pupford wasn't there), and bringing back some surprising intelligence concerning the bonnet.

The extensive preparations being completed on the day before the holidays, an unanimous entreaty was preferred to Miss Pupford by the pupil-mind--finding expression through Miss Pupford's assistant--that she would deign to appear in all her splendour. Miss Pupford consenting, presented a lovely spectacle. And although the oldest pupil was barely thirteen, every one of the six became in two minutes perfect in the shape, cut, colour, price, and quality, of every article Miss Pupford wore.

Thus delightfully ushered in, the holidays began. Five of the six pupils kissed little Kitty Kimmeens twenty times over (round total, one hundred times, for she was very popular), and so went home. Miss Kitty Kimmeens remained behind, for her relations and friends were all in India, far away. A self-helpful steady little child is Miss Kitty Kimmeens: a dimpled child too, and a loving.

So, the great marriage-day came, and Miss Pupford, quite as much fluttered as any bride could be (G! thought Miss Kitty Kimmeens), went away, splendid to behold, in the carriage that was sent for her. But not Miss Pupford only went away; for Miss Pupford's assistant went away with her, on a dutiful visit to an aged uncle--though surely the venerable gentleman couldn't live in the gallery of the church where the marriage was to be, thought Miss Kitty Kimmeens--and yet Miss Pupford's assistant had let out that she was going there. Where the cook was going, didn't appear, but she generally conveyed to Miss Kimmeens that she was bound, rather against her will, on a pilgrimage to perform some pious office that rendered new ribbons necessary to her best bonnet, and also sandals to her shoes.

"So you see," said the housemaid, when they were all gone, "there's nobody left in the house but you and me, Miss Kimmeens."

"Nobody else," said Miss Kitty Kimmeens, shaking her curls a little sadly. "Nobody!"

"And you wouldn't like your Bella to go too; would you, Miss Kimmeens?" said the housemaid. (She being Bella.)

"N-no," answered little Miss Kimmeens.

"Your poor Bella is forced to stay with you, whether she likes it or not; ain't she, Miss Kimmeens?"

"***Don't*** you like it?" inquired Kitty.

"Why, you're such a darling, Miss, that it would be unkind of your Bella to make objections. Yet my brother-in-law has been took unexpected bad by this morning's post. And your poor Bella is much attached to him, letting alone her favourite sister, Miss Kimmeens."

"Is he very ill?" asked little Kitty.

"Your poor Bella has her fears so, Miss Kimmeens," returned the housemaid, with her apron at her eyes. "It was but his inside, it is true, but it might mount, and the doctor said that if it mounted he wouldn't answer." Here the housemaid was so overcome that Kitty administered the only comfort she had ready: which was a kiss.

"If it hadn't been for disappointing Cook, dear Miss Kimmeens," said the housemaid, "your Bella would have asked her to stay with you. For Cook is sweet company, Miss Kimmeens, much more so than your own poor Bella."

"But you are very nice, Bella."

"Your Bella could wish to be so, Miss Kimmeens," returned the housemaid, "but she knows full well that it do not lay in her power this day."

With which despondent conviction, the housemaid drew a heavy sigh, and shook her head, and dropped it on one side.

"If it had been anyways right to disappoint Cook," she pursued, in a contemplative and abstracted manner, "it might have been so easy done! I could have got to my brother-in-law's, and had the best part of the day there, and got back, long before our ladies come home at night, and neither the one nor the other of them need never have known it. Not that Miss Pupford would at all object, but that it might put her out, being tender-hearted. Hows'ever, your own poor Bella, Miss Kimmeens," said the housemaid, rousing herself, "is forced to stay with you, and you're a precious love, if not a liberty."

"Bella," said little Kitty, after a short silence.

"Call your own poor Bella, your Bella, dear," the housemaid besought her.

"My Bella, then."

"Bless your considerate heart!" said the housemaid.

"If you would not mind leaving me, I should not mind being left. I am not afraid to stay in the house alone. And you need not be uneasy on my account, for I would be very careful to do no harm."

"O! As to harm, you more than sweetest, if not a liberty," exclaimed the housemaid, in a rapture, "your Bella could trust you anywhere, being so steady, and so answerable. The oldest head in this house (me and Cook says), but for its bright hair, is Miss Kimmeens. But no, I will not leave you; for you would think your Bella unkind."

"But if you are my Bella, you **must** go," returned the child.

"Must I?" said the housemaid, rising, on the whole with alacrity. "What must be, must be, Miss Kimmeens. Your own poor Bella acts according, though unwilling. But go or stay, your own poor Bella loves you, Miss Kimmeens."

It was certainly go, and not stay, for within five minutes Miss Kimmeens's own poor Bella--so much improved in point of spirits as to have grown almost sanguine on the subject of her brother-in-law--went her way, in apparel that seemed to have been expressly prepared for some festive occasion. Such are the changes of this fleeting world, and so short-sighted are we poor mortals!

When the house door closed with a bang and a shake, it seemed to Miss Kimmeens to be a very heavy house door, shutting her up in a wilderness of a house. But, Miss Kimmeens being, as before stated, of a self-reliant and methodical character, presently began to parcel out the long summer-day before her.

And first she thought she would go all over the house, to make quite sure that nobody with a great-coat on and a carving-knife in it, had got under one of the beds or into one of the cupboards. Not that she had ever before been troubled by the image of anybody armed with a great-coat and a carving-knife, but that it seemed to have been shaken into existence by the shake and the bang of the great street-door, reverberating through the solitary house. So, little Miss Kimmeens looked under the five empty beds of the five departed pupils, and looked, under her own bed, and looked under Miss Pupford's bed, and looked under Miss Pupford's assistants bed. And when she had done this, and was making the tour of the cupboards, the disagreeable thought came into her young head, What a very alarming thing it would be to find somebody with a mask on, like Guy Fawkes, hiding bolt upright in a corner and pretending not to be alive! However, Miss Kimmeens having finished her inspection without making any such uncomfortable discovery, sat down in her tidy little manner to needlework, and began stitching away at a great rate.

The silence all about her soon grew very oppressive, and the more so because of the odd inconsistency that the more silent it was, the more noises there were. The noise of her own needle and thread as she stitched, was infinitely louder in her ears than the stitching of all the six pupils, and of Miss Pupford, and of Miss Pupford's assistant, all stitching away at once on a highly emulative afternoon. Then, the schoolroom clock conducted itself in a way in which it had never conducted itself before--fell lame, somehow, and yet persisted in running on as hard and as loud as it could: the consequence of which behaviour was, that it staggered among the minutes in a state of the greatest confusion, and knocked them about in all directions without appearing to get on with its regular work. Perhaps this alarmed the stairs; but be that as it might, they began to creak in a most unusual manner, and then the furniture began to crack, and then poor little Miss Kimmeens, not liking the furtive aspect of things in general, began to sing as she stitched. But, it was not her own voice that she heard--it was somebody else making believe to be Kitty, and singing excessively flat, without any heart--so as that would never mend matters, she left off again.

By-and-by the stitching became so palpable a failure that Miss Kitty Kimmeens folded her work neatly, and put it away in its box, and gave it up. Then the question arose about reading. But no; the book that was so delightful when there was somebody she loved for her eyes to fall on when they rose from the page, had not more heart in it than her own singing now. The book went to its shelf as the needlework had gone to its box, and, since something **must** be done--thought the child, "I'll go put my room to rights."

She shared her room with her dearest little friend among the other five pupils, and why then should she now conceive a lurking dread of the little friend's bedstead? But she did. There was a stealthy air about its innocent white curtains, and there were even dark hints of a dead girl lying under the coverlet. The great want of human company, the great need of a human face, began now to express itself in the facility with which the furniture put on strange exaggerated resemblances to human looks. A chair with a menacing frown was horribly out of temper in a corner; a most vicious chest of drawers snarled at her from between the windows. It was no relief to escape from those monsters to the looking- glass, for the reflection said, "What? Is that you all alone there? How you stare!" And the background was all a great void stare as well.

The day dragged on, dragging Kitty with it very slowly by the hair of her head, until it was time to eat. There were good provisions in the pantry, but their right flavour and relish had evaporated with the five pupils, and Miss Pupford, and Miss Pupford's assistant, and the cook and housemaid. Where was the use of laying the cloth symmetrically for one small guest, who had gone on ever since the morning growing smaller and smaller, while the empty house had gone on swelling larger and larger? The very Grace came out wrong, for who were "we" who were going to receive and be thankful? So, Miss Kimmeens was *not* thankful, and found herself taking her dinner in very slovenly style--gobbling it up, in short, rather after the manner of the lower animals, not to particularise the pigs.

But, this was by no means the worst of the change wrought out in the naturally loving and cheery little creature as the solitary day wore on. She began to brood and be suspicious. She discovered that she was full of wrongs and injuries. All the people she knew, got tainted by her lonely thoughts and turned bad.

It was all very well for Papa, a widower in India, to send her home to be educated, and to pay a handsome round sum every year for her to Miss Pupford, and to write charming letters to his darling little daughter; but what did he care for her being left by herself, when he was (as no doubt he always was) enjoying himself in company from morning till night? Perhaps he only sent her here, after all, to get her out of the way. It looked like it--looked like it to-day, that is, for she had never dreamed of such a thing before.

And this old pupil who was being married. It was unsupportably conceited and selfish in the old pupil to be married. She was very vain, and very glad to show off; but it was highly probable that she wasn't pretty; and even if she were pretty (which Miss Kimmeens now totally denied), she had no business to be married; and, even if marriage were conceded, she had no business to ask Miss Pupford to her wedding. As to Miss Pupford, she was too old to go to any wedding. She ought to know that. She had much better attend to her business. She had thought she looked nice in the morning, but she didn't look nice. She was a stupid old thing. G was another stupid old thing. Miss Pupford's assistant was another. They were all stupid old things together.

More than that: it began to be obvious that this was a plot. They had said to one another, "Never mind Kitty; you get off, and I'll get off; and we'll leave Kitty to look after herself. Who cares for her?" To be sure they were right in that question; for who *did* care for her, a poor little lonely thing against whom they all planned and plotted? Nobody, nobody! Here Kitty sobbed.

At all other times she was the pet of the whole house, and loved her five companions in return with a child's tenderest and most ingenuous attachment; but now, the five companions put on ugly colours, and appeared for the first time under a sullen cloud. There they were, all at their homes that day, being made much of, being taken out, being spoilt and made disagreeable, and caring nothing for her. It was like their artful selfishness always to tell her when they came back, under pretence of confidence and friendship, all those details about where they had been, and what they had done and seen, and how often they had said, "O! If we had only darling little Kitty here!" Here indeed! I dare say! When they came back after the holidays, they were used to being received by Kitty, and to saying that coming to Kitty was like coming to another home. Very well then, why did they go away? If the meant it, why did they go away? Let them answer that. But they didn't mean it, and couldn't answer that, and they didn't tell the truth, and people who didn't tell the truth were hateful. When they came back next time, they should be received in a new manner; they should be avoided and shunned.

And there, the while she sat all alone revolving how ill she was used, and how much better she was than the people who were not alone, the wedding breakfast was going on: no question of it! With a nasty great bride-cake, and with those ridiculous orange-flowers, and with that conceited bride, and that hideous bridegroom, and those heartless bridesmaids, and Miss Pupford stuck up at the table! They thought they were enjoying themselves, but it would come home to them one day to have thought so. They would all be dead in a few years, let them enjoy themselves ever so much. It was a religious comfort to know that.

It was such a comfort to know it, that little Miss Kitty Kimmeens suddenly sprang from the chair in which she had been musing in a corner, and cried out, "O those envious thoughts are not mine, O this wicked creature isn't me! Help me, somebody! I go wrong, alone by my weak self! Help me, anybody!"

* * * * *

"--Miss Kimmeens is not a professed philosopher, sir," said Mr. Traveller, presenting her at the barred window, and smoothing her shining hair, "but I apprehend there was some tincture of philosophy in her words, and in the prompt action with which she followed them. That action was, to emerge from her unnatural solitude, and look abroad for wholesome sympathy, to bestow and to receive. Her footsteps strayed to this gate, bringing her here by chance, as an apposite contrast to you. The child came out, sir. If you have the wisdom to learn from a child (but I doubt it, for that requires more wisdom than one in your condition would seem to possess), you cannot do better than imitate the child, and come out too--from that very demoralising hutch of yours."

CHAPTER VII--PICKING UP THE TINKER

It was now sunset. The Hermit had betaken himself to his bed of cinders half an hour ago, and lying on it in his blanket and skewer with his back to the window, took not the smallest heed of the appeal addressed to him.

All that had been said for the last two hours, had been said to a tinkling accompaniment performed by the Tinker, who had got to work upon some villager's pot or kettle, and was working briskly outside. This music still continuing, seemed to put it into Mr. Traveller's mind to have another word or two with the Tinker. So, holding Miss Kimmeens (with whom he was now on the most friendly terms) by the hand, he went out at the gate to where the Tinker was seated at his work on the patch of grass on the opposite side of the road, with his wallet of tools open before him, and his little fire smoking.

"I am glad to see you employed," said Mr. Traveller.

"I am glad to *be* employed," returned the Tinker, looking up as he put the finishing touches to his job. "But why are you glad?"

"I thought you were a lazy fellow when I saw you this morning."

"I was only disgusted," said the Tinker.

"Do you mean with the fine weather?"

"With the fine weather?" repeated the Tinker, staring.

"You told me you were not particular as to weather, and I thought--"

"Ha, ha! How should such as me get on, if we *was* particular as to weather? We must take it as it comes, and make the best of it. There's something good in all weathers. If it don't happen to be good for my work to-day, it's good for some other man's to-day, and will come round to me to-morrow. We must all live."

"Pray shake hands," said Mr. Traveller.

"Take care, sir," was the Tinker's caution, as he reached up his hand in surprise; "the black comes off."

"I am glad of it," said Mr. Traveller. "I have been for several hours among other black that does not come off."

"You are speaking of Tom in there?"

"Yes."

"Well now," said the Tinker, blowing the dust off his job: which was finished. "Ain't it enough to disgust a pig, if he could give his mind to it?"

"If he could give his mind to it," returned the other, smiling, "the probability is that he wouldn't be a pig."

"There you clench the nail," returned the Tinker. "Then what's to be said for Tom?"

"Truly, very little."

"Truly nothing you mean, sir," said the Tinker, as he put away his tools.

"A better answer, and (I freely acknowledge) my meaning. I infer that he was the cause of your disgust?"

"Why, look'ee here, sir," said the Tinker, rising to his feet, and wiping his face on the corner of his black apron energetically; "I leave you to judge!--I ask you!-- Last night I has a job that needs to be done in the night, and I works all night. Well, there's nothing in that. But this morning I comes along this road here, looking for a sunny and soft spot to sleep in, and I sees this desolation and ruination. I've lived myself in desolation and ruination; I knows many a fellow-creetur that's forced to live life long in desolation and ruination; and I sits me down and takes pity on it, as I casts my eyes about. Then comes up the long-winded one as I told you of, from that gate, and spins himself out like a silkworm concerning the Donkey (if my Donkey at home will excuse me) as has made it all--made it of his own choice! And tells me, if you please, of his likewise choosing to go ragged and naked, and grimy- -maskerading, mountebanking, in what is the real hard lot of thousands and thou- sands! Why, then I say it's a unbearable and nonsensical piece of inconsistency, and I'm disgusted. I'm ashamed and disgusted!"

"I wish you would come and look at him," said Mr. Traveller, clapping the Tinker on the shoulder.

"Not I, sir," he rejoined. "I ain't a going to flatter him up by looking at him!"

"But he is asleep."

"Are you sure he is asleep?" asked the Tinker, with an unwilling air, as he shouldered his wallet.

"Sure."

"Then I'll look at him for a quarter of a minute," said the Tinker, "since you so much wish it; but not a moment longer."

They all three went back across the road; and, through the barred window, by the dying glow of the sunset coming in at the gate--which the child held open for its admission--he could be pretty clearly discerned lying on his bed.

"You see him?" asked Mr. Traveller.

"Yes," returned the Tinker, "and he's worse than I thought him."

Mr. Traveller then whispered in few words what he had done since morning; and asked the Tinker what he thought of that?

"I think," returned the Tinker, as he turned from the window, "that you've wasted a day on him."

"I think so too; though not, I hope, upon myself. Do you happen to be going anywhere near the Peal of Bells?"

"That's my direct way, sir," said the Tinker.

"I invite you to supper there. And as I learn from this young lady that she goes some three-quarters of a mile in the same direction, we will drop her on the road, and we will spare time to keep her company at her garden gate until her own Bella comes home."

So, Mr. Traveller, and the child, and the Tinker, went along very amicably in the sweet-scented evening; and the moral with which the Tinker dismissed the subject was, that he said in his trade that metal that rotted for want of use, had better be left to rot, and couldn't rot too soon, considering how much true metal rotted from over-use and hard service.

NOTES

{1} Dickens didn't write chapters 2 to 5 and they are omitted in this edition.

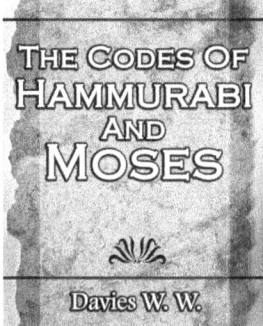

The Codes Of Hammurabi And Moses
W. W. Davies

QTY

The discovery of the Hammurabi Code is one of the greatest achievements of archaeology, and is of paramount interest, not only to the student of the Bible, but also to all those interested in ancient history...

Religion   ISBN: *1-59462-338-4*   **Pages:132**
MSRP $12.95

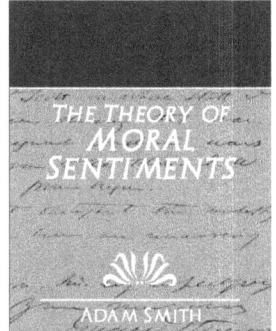

The Theory of Moral Sentiments
Adam Smith

QTY

This work from 1749. contains original theories of conscience amd moral judgment and it is the foundation for systemof morals.

Philosophy   ISBN: *1-59462-777-0*   **Pages:536**
MSRP $19.95

Jessica's First Prayer
Hesba Stretton

QTY

In a screened and secluded corner of one of the many railway-bridges which span the streets of London there could be seen a few years ago, from five o'clock every morning until half past eight, a tidily set-out coffee-stall, consisting of a trestle and board, upon which stood two large tin cans, with a small fire of charcoal burning under each so as to keep the coffee boiling during the early hours of the morning when the work-people were thronging into the city on their way to their daily toil...

Childrens   ISBN: *1-59462-373-2*   **Pages:84**
MSRP $9.95

My Life and Work
Henry Ford

QTY

Henry Ford revolutionized the world with his implementation of mass production for the Model T automobile. Gain valuable business insight into his life and work with his own auto-biography... "We have only started on our development of our country we have not as yet, with all our talk of wonderful progress, done more than scratch the surface. The progress has been wonderful enough but..."

Biographies/   ISBN: *1-59462-198-5*   **Pages:300**
MSRP $21.95

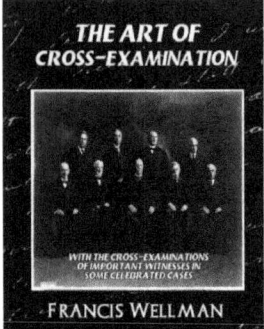

The Art of Cross-Examination
Francis Wellman

QTY

I presume it is the experience of every author, after his first book is published upon an important subject, to be almost overwhelmed with a wealth of ideas and illustrations which could readily have been included in his book, and which to his own mind, at least, seem to make a second edition inevitable. Such certainly was the case with me; and when the first edition had reached its sixth impression in five months, I rejoiced to learn that it seemed to my publishers that the book had met with a sufficiently favorable reception to justify a second and considerably enlarged edition. ..

Reference   ISBN: *1-59462-647-2*

Pages:412

MSRP $19.95

On the Duty of Civil Disobedience
Henry David Thoreau

QTY

Thoreau wrote his famous essay, On the Duty of Civil Disobedience, as a protest against an unjust but popular war and the immoral but popular institution of slave-owning. He did more than write—he declined to pay his taxes, and was hauled off to gaol in consequence. Who can say how much this refusal of his hastened the end of the war and of slavery ?

Law   ISBN: *1-59462-747-9*

Pages:48

MSRP $7.45

Dream Psychology Psychoanalysis for Beginners
Sigmund Freud

QTY

Sigmund Freud, born Sigismund Schlomo Freud (May 6, 1856 - September 23, 1939), was a Jewish-Austrian neurologist and psychiatrist who co-founded the psychoanalytic school of psychology. Freud is best known for his theories of the unconscious mind, especially involving the mechanism of repression; his redefinition of sexual desire as mobile and directed towards a wide variety of objects; and his therapeutic techniques, especially his understanding of transference in the therapeutic relationship and the presumed value of dreams as sources of insight into unconscious desires.

Psychology   ISBN: *1-59462-905-6*

Pages:196

MSRP $15.45

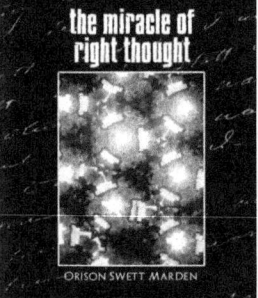

The Miracle of Right Thought
Orison Swett Marden

QTY

Believe with all of your heart that you will do what you were made to do. When the mind has once formed the habit of holding cheerful, happy, prosperous pictures, it will not be easy to form the opposite habit. It does not matter how improbable or how far away this realization may see, or how dark the prospects may be, if we visualize them as best we can, as vividly as possible, hold tenaciously to them and vigorously struggle to attain them, they will gradually become actualized, realized in the life. But a desire, a longing without endeavor, a yearning abandoned or held indifferently will vanish without realization.

Self Help   ISBN: *1-59462-644-8*

Pages:360

MSRP $25.45

The Rosicrucian Cosmo-Conception Mystic Christianity by *Max Heindel* ISBN: *1-59462-188-8* **$38.95**
The Rosicrucian Cosmo-conception is not dogmatic, neither does it appeal to any other authority than the reason of the student. It is: not controversial, but is: sent forth in the, hope that it may help to clear... New Age/Religion Pages 646

Abandonment To Divine Providence by *Jean-Pierre de Caussade* ISBN: *1-59462-228-0* **$25.95**
"The Rev. Jean Pierre de Caussade was one of the most remarkable spiritual writers of the Society of Jesus in France in the 18th Century. His death took place at Toulouse in 1751. His works have gone through many editions and have been republished... Inspirational/Religion Pages 400

Mental Chemistry by *Charles Haanel* ISBN: *1-59462-192-6* **$23.95**
Mental Chemistry allows the change of material conditions by combining and appropriately utilizing the power of the mind. Much like applied chemistry creates something new and unique out of careful combinations of chemicals the mastery of mental chemistry... New Age Pages 354

The Letters of Robert Browning and Elizabeth Barret Barrett 1845-1846 vol II ISBN: *1-59462-193-4* **$35.95**
by *Robert Browning* and *Elizabeth Barrett* Biographies Pages 596

Gleanings In Genesis (volume I) by *Arthur W. Pink* ISBN: *1-59462-130-6* **$27.45**
Appropriately has Genesis been termed "the seed plot of the Bible" for in it we have, in germ form, almost all of the great doctrines which are afterwards fully developed in the books of Scripture which follow... Religion/Inspirational Pages 420

The Master Key by *L. W. de Laurence* ISBN: *1-59462-001-6* **$30.95**
In no branch of human knowledge has there been a more lively increase of the spirit of research during the past few years than in the study of Psychology, Concentration and Mental Discipline. The requests for authentic lessons in Thought Control, Mental Discipline and... New Age/Business Pages 422

The Lesser Key Of Solomon Goetia by *L. W. de Laurence* ISBN: *1-59462-092-X* **$9.95**
This translation of the first book of the "Lernegton" which is now for the first time made accessible to students of Talismanic Magic was done, after careful collation and edition, from numerous Ancient Manuscripts in Hebrew, Latin, and French... New Age/Occult Pages 92

Rubaiyat Of Omar Khayyam by *Edward Fitzgerald* ISBN:*1-59462-332-5* **$13.95**
Edward Fitzgerald, whom the world has already learned, in spite of his own efforts to remain within the shadow of anonymity, to look upon as one of the rarest poets of the century, was born at Bredfield, in Suffolk, on the 31st of March, 1809. He was the third son of John Purcell... Music Pages 172

Ancient Law by *Henry Maine* ISBN: *1-59462-128-4* **$29.95**
The chief object of the following pages is to indicate some of the earliest ideas of mankind, as they are reflected in Ancient Law, and to point out the relation of those ideas to modern thought. Religiom/History Pages 452

Far-Away Stories by *William J. Locke* ISBN: *1-59462-129-2* **$19.45**
"Good wine needs no bush, but a collection of mixed vintages does. And this book is just such a collection. Some of the stories I do not want to remain buried for ever in the museum files of dead magazine-numbers an author's not unpardonable vanity..." Fiction Pages 272

Life of David Crockett by *David Crockett* ISBN: *1-59462-250-7* **$27.45**
"Colonel David Crockett was one of the most remarkable men of the times in which he lived. Born in humble life, but gifted with a strong will, an indomitable courage, and unremitting perseverance... Biographies/New Age Pages 424

Lip-Reading by *Edward Nitchie* ISBN: *1-59462-206-X* **$25.95**
Edward B. Nitchie, founder of the New York School for the Hard of Hearing, now the Nitchie School of Lip-Reading, Inc, wrote "LIP-READING Principles and Practice". The development and perfecting of this meritorious work on lip-reading was an undertaking... How-to Pages 400

A Handbook of Suggestive Therapeutics, Applied Hypnotism, Psychic Science ISBN: *1-59462-214-0* **$24.95**
by *Henry Munro* Health/New Age/Health/Self-help Pages 376

A Doll's House: and Two Other Plays by *Henrik Ibsen* ISBN: *1-59462-112-8* **$19.95**
Henrik Ibsen created this classic when in revolutionary 1848 Rome. Introducing some striking concepts in playwriting for the realist genre, this play has been studied the world over. Fiction/Classics/Plays 308

The Light of Asia by *sir Edwin Arnold* ISBN: *1-59462-204-3* **$13.95**
In this poetic masterpiece, Edwin Arnold describes the life and teachings of Buddha. The man who was to become known as Buddha to the world was born as Prince Gautama of India but he rejected the worldly riches and abandoned the reigns of power when... Religion/History/Biographies Pages 170

The Complete Works of Guy de Maupassant by *Guy de Maupassant* ISBN: *1-59462-157-8* **$16.95**
"For days and days, nights and nights, I had dreamed of that first kiss which was to consecrate our engagement, and I knew not on what spot I should put my lips..." Fiction/Classics Pages 240

The Art of Cross-Examination by *Francis L. Wellman* ISBN: *1-59462-309-0* **$26.95**
Written by a renowned trial lawyer, Wellman imparts his experience and uses case studies to explain how to use psychology to extract desired information through questioning. How-to/Science/Reference Pages 408

Answered or Unanswered? by *Louisa Vaughan* ISBN: *1-59462-248-5* **$10.95**
Miracles of Faith in China Religion Pages 112

The Edinburgh Lectures on Mental Science (1909) by *Thomas* ISBN: *1-59462-008-3* **$11.95**
This book contains the substance of a course of lectures recently given by the writer in the Queen Street Hail, Edinburgh. Its purpose is to indicate the Natural Principles governing the relation between Mental Action and Material Conditions... New Age/Psychology Pages 148

Ayesha by *H. Rider Haggard* ISBN: *1-59462-301-5* **$24.95**
Verily and indeed it is the unexpected that happens! Probably if there was one person upon the earth from whom the Editor of this, and of a certain previous history, did not expect to hear again... Classics Pages 380

Ayala's Angel by *Anthony Trollope* ISBN: *1-59462-352-X* **$29.95**
The two girls were both pretty, but Lucy who was twenty-one who supposed to be simple and comparatively unattractive, whereas Ayala was credited, as her Bombwhat romantic name might show, with poetic charm and a taste for romance. Ayala when her father died was nineteen... Fiction Pages 484

The American Commonwealth by *James Bryce* ISBN: *1-59462-286-8* **$34.45**
An interpretation of American democratic political theory. It examines political mechanics and society from the perspective of Scotsman James Bryce Politics Pages 572

Stories of the Pilgrims by *Margaret P. Pumphrey* ISBN: *1-59462-116-0* **$17.95**
This book explores pilgrims religious oppression in England as well as their escape to Holland and eventual crossing to America on the Mayflower, and their early days in New England... History Pages 268

QTY

The Fasting Cure *by Sinclair Upton*
ISBN: *1-59462-222-1* **$13.95**

In the Cosmopolitan Magazine for May, 1910, and in the Contemporary Review (London) for April, 1910, I published an article dealing with my experiences in fasting. I have written a great many magazine articles, but never one which attracted so much attention... New Age/Self Help/Health Pages 164

Hebrew Astrology *by Sepharial*
ISBN: *1-59462-308-2* **$13.45**

In these days of advanced thinking it is a matter of common observation that we have left many of the old landmarks behind and that we are now pressing forward to greater heights and to a wider horizon than that which represented the mind-content of our progenitors... Astrology Pages 144

Thought Vibration or The Law of Attraction in the Thought World
by William Walker Atkinson
ISBN: *1-59462-127-6* **$12.95**

Psychology/Religion Pages 144

Optimism *by Helen Keller*
ISBN: *1-59462-108-X* **$15.95**

Helen Keller was blind, deaf, and mute since 19 months old, yet famously learned how to overcome these handicaps, communicate with the world, and spread her lectures promoting optimism. An inspiring read for everyone... Biographies/Inspirational Pages 84

Sara Crewe *by Frances Burnett*
ISBN: *1-59462-360-0* **$9.45**

In the first place, Miss Minchin lived in London. Her home was a large, dull, tall one, in a large, dull square, where all the houses were alike, and all the sparrows were alike, and where all the door-knockers made the same heavy sound... Childrens/Classic Pages 88

The Autobiography of Benjamin Franklin *by Benjamin Franklin*
ISBN: *1-59462-135-7* **$24.95**

The Autobiography of Benjamin Franklin has probably been more extensively read than any other American historical work, and no other book of its kind has had such ups and downs of fortune. Franklin lived for many years in England, where he was agent... Biographies/History Pages 332

Name	
Email	
Telephone	
Address	
City, State ZIP	

☐ **Credit Card**   ☐ **Check / Money Order**

Credit Card Number	
Expiration Date	
Signature	

Please Mail to: Book Jungle
PO Box 2226
Champaign, IL 61825
or Fax to: 630-214-0564

ORDERING INFORMATION

web*: www.bookjungle.com*
email*: sales@bookjungle.com*
fax*: 630-214-0564*
mail*: Book Jungle PO Box 2226 Champaign, IL 61825*
or PayPal *to sales@bookjungle.com*

Please contact us for bulk discounts

DIRECT-ORDER TERMS

**20% Discount if You Order
Two or More Books**
Free Domestic Shipping!
Accepted: Master Card, Visa,
Discover, American Express

www.ingramcontent.com/pod-product-compliance
Lightning Source LLC
Chambersburg PA
CBHW081204170626
46813CB00009B/3315